The Mouse with the Broken Tail

By Dan Shutters

Illustrations by Sharon Shiffler

The Mouse with the Broken Tail

SECOND SUNBURY PRESS EDITION
Printed in the United States of America
February 2013

ISBN 978-1-62006-189-3

Published by:
Sunbury Press, Inc.
50-A West Main St.
Mechanicsburg, PA   17055

www.sunburypress.com

Mechanicsburg, Pennsylvania   USA

Dedication

To those who were children in the congregations I have served who challenged me to always try to do better.

To those who still are children in the heart.

Thank you to Sharon Shiffler for providing the illustrations for this story.

Chapter 1

Once upon a time, there was a mouse who walked freely inside a house, unafraid of the cat that lived there, but a trap made of wood and steel lay waiting for him. Once the trap was sprung, it would kill him or at least make him a prisoner. That had been the fate of many generations of mice who had yielded to the tempting smells of the trap. Now to each new generation of mice these words of wisdom and warning were spoken: "Delicious smells are often deadly. Eating the cheese will cost your life."

The trap was tempting. As soon as its bait became hard and stale, new bait replaced it. Many cheeses had been placed there: Swiss, American, and both sharp and mild varieties of Cheddar. Their deadly aromas floated through the air.

The trap was an evil thing for a mouse. It lay waiting. An unmoving, coiled spring waited only for one fatal movement to bring it into action. Unlike cats it never moved, which made it seem harmless. Everyday the mice would pass by the trap. As they went they would repeat the words of their ancestors, ". . . Eating the cheese will cost your life."

The trap takes its victims one by one. It waits along the edge of a wall not knowing who its victim will be, but knowing that there will be a victim. It sits along the wall's edge because all mice are afraid of open places. Mice use their whiskers to feel the wall in the darkness. Being able to touch makes a mouse feel less lonely. Here the trap waits, unmoving and silent, for a mouse, any mouse to make one misstep.

Temptation catches many in its trap. It doesn't care about names or personalities, or the good deeds its victims have done. It has no respect for history. Those who are caught in its grip ask, "Why me? What did I do to deserve this? It answers only with silence.

One mouse named Sam had heard stories of the trap. He had gone to see the temptation and returned unharmed. Sam had smelled the delicious aroma of cheddar. He had been a whisker away from the temptation and was still unharmed. The scent lingered in his memory and he was lured back to the trap. Every time Sam returned to the coiled spring trap and came away safe, his courage was strengthened. Still, he had not yet taken the bait. He could still hear the words of warning in his mind, "Delicious smells are often deadly. Eating the cheese will cost your life."

One night Sam climbed up onto the wooden trap. Carefully, and ever so lightly, he touched the bait. Nothing happened. Sam could hardly believe it. The stories of his ancestors were false. He boasted to the other mice of his feat. He announced to them, "A mouse can walk into the trap and not be harmed. Perhaps the trap was deadly once, but now the spring must be rusted. This thing we have called evil, is but a frozen relic of the past. It is harmless."

Encouraged by his own squeaking, Sam dismissed the warning words of his ancestors and returned to the trap. He had convinced himself that the bait was there for the taking. He was going to eat it. His mouth opened to take the forbidden food.

The trap that had waited so long, loosed its deadly spring. Sam was about to be caught. Sam was going to learn that warnings are given to protect the inexperienced.

Chapter 2

Now, Sam was quicker than most mice. In spite of his boasting, and because he was still a nervous mouse, he kept an eye open for any sign of movement from the trap. At the last moment, he changed his mind. The advice of his ancestors, "Delicious smells can be deadly," made him pull back from the cheese. He turned and stepped off the trap, only to have his tail tap the bait. The steel bar swung into action. Only Sam's tail was caught, and it was stuck. He could not free himself. He tugged and pulled with all his might, but wherever he went the trap went. He pulled the trap around the room. He wanted to go back

to his home, but the trap wouldn't fit through the hole in the wall. He backed out and ran around the room again. The trap sapped the strength from him. Exhausted, he collapsed on the floor. Sam knew his fate was sealed.

Sam was angry at the trap that imprisoned him. He was angry at himself for not listening to the words of his ancestors. He was hurt, confused and hungry. The irony of it all was that he hadn't even enjoyed the cheese that had caused him the pain. Sam felt cheated all around.

For Sam, this might have been the end of the story, but there was good news. A Being came into his life. This Being was something Sam had never seen before. He had been told that the world in which he lived had been made by this Great Being. The

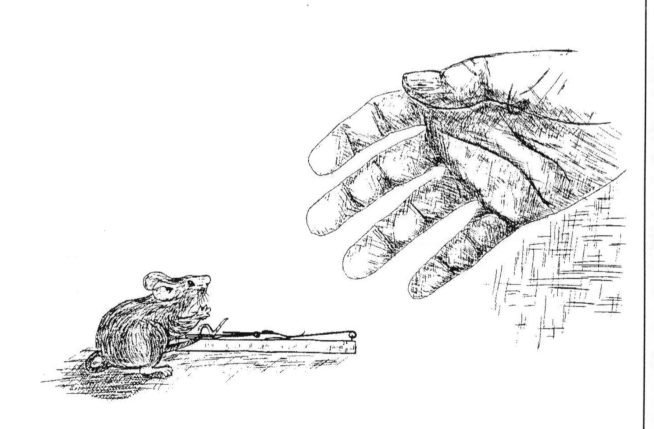

walls, floors, and ceiling were all designed by the Being. All the good things the mice enjoyed were the result of this Being's creation. Still, Sam had never before encountered the Being in the rafters where he made his home.

The trap, as evil as it was, had been a fearful thing to the mice, but it was small in comparison to this Being whose trap now held Sam. The Being was as large as a thousand traps. Sam who before had only been terrified, was struck with awe in the presence of the Great Being.

The Being towered over him. He reached down and picked up the trap that held Sam. Because Sam was caught by the trap, he felt himself being lifted high into the air. The Being said, "I have listened to you walking between the walls at night, and I know the place you call home. I gave you the name, Sam. Now we meet, face to face."

Chapter 3

Then a wondrous thing was done. Sam was taken to a place called Outside. He had never before seen a world like this. There were trees, green grass, and a blinding light whose warmth shone down on him. Being held upside down by the tail was not the right way to view a new world however, and Sam didn't have time to appreciate all that was around him. He was just a little mouse, and he was not used to being Outside. He was very afraid and looked for a place to hide. Out of the corner of his eye, he saw a refuge for himself, if he could ever get loose from the trap: a woodpile. The logs looked like a home, a place where a small mouse could feel safe and secure.

The Being drew near to the woodpile and lowered the trap. Because Sam was attached to the trap, he was lowered too. As his feet touched the ground, the Being spoke, "Little one, I shall always know you by your broken tail. Be not afraid. I am setting you free."

A hand released the steel jaws of the Evil that held him. Sam tumbled to the ground and rushed for cover. As he trembled within his new, log home, he heard the voice add, "Go in peace."

To this day, Sam is recognized by his broken tail. If you could talk with him he would tell you that he now believes in Evil. He would tell you of the trap with its tempting aromas and its deadly consequence. He would recite the words he once ignored, "Delicious smells are often deadly. Eating the cheese will cost you your life."

Most of all, Sam would whisper of a Great Being, more powerful than the trap that had imprisoned him. With awe, Sam would speak in hushed tones of a Being who knows how he suffered, who cares for him, who released him from prison, and who gave him a greater freedom than he had ever known before.

Sam thought he was in a mouse heaven. All the comforts that he could think of surrounded him. What more could a mouse want?

Chapter 4

Sam was in the woodpile. The woodpile was a terrific place to be. Sam thought it was a lot like heaven. The scent of freshly cut cherry wood wrapped itself around him. Sawdust littered the ground to form a soft bed.

The grass seed was a new treat for Sam, and there were berries he had never tasted before. They formed a mouse feast. Sam had all kinds of creature comforts, but he was lonely.

Sam knew that back in the house, his family would be gathering in a nest made from pink ceiling insulation. They had problems to deal with, but Sam had enjoyed listening to and telling stories of how generations of mice had overcome their hardships. Outside among the finest sawdust and berries, Sam was lonely.

Heaven is more than things we can feel and taste. It is being with those you love and who love you in return.

Sam peered out from the woodpile and longingly gazed back toward the house where his family was. The longer he looked, the more he knew he would have to go back into that house. The next evening, he made his decision. As he scurried back to the house, Sam spotted a large round hole that seemed to lead directly into the house. "I'm going home," Sam thought.

Chapter 5

Having decided that fellow creatures are more important than his own comfort, Sam decided to go back to his home. But getting in the house was not going to be easy. Then Sam inspected the drain pipe, and it looked like the perfect entrance to the house. Getting back into the house was going to be a piece of cake. (Oops, make that a piece of cheese.)

Sam entered the dark tunnel. Before he knew it, the path started to curve upward. It was dark, and although he couldn't tell how far it stretched, this looked like the perfect solution. He tried to climb up the pipe. A running start was what he needed. He backed up to gather speed. He ran through the tube as fast as he could and when he hit the curve he started the upward journey into the blackness, but it was not enough. He backed up and started into the pipe again. He went even higher up the tube. This time he ran into a leaf blockage. He tried to hang onto a leaf, but it came loose, and down he slid on this leaf turned toboggan. Amazed, but not discouraged, Sam took a third running start into the pipe. Up, up he went until the blockage stopped him. Again, a leaf loosened from the pack and down he slid. Sam might have enjoyed the experience, if he were only in it for the sled ride, but he had another goal in mind. He soon realized that the way that had seemed so easy at first was not going to be the answer to his problem after all.

A sad, lonely mouse cried himself to sleep that night amidst the smell of cherry wood and pine. It looked like he was going to live out his life surrounded by all the good things he could want, but missing the love of his family that he needed.

In the morning, Sam couldn't help thinking again about how he could get into the house. Then he saw something he had not noticed before. There was sawdust sitting in little piles on the ground. He looked around to see what was creating the sawdust

and saw a colony of ants eating into the wood beside him. There were also large black carpenter bees drilling round holes in the wood above him. Could the ants and bees help a mouse? Would they?

Chapter 6

Sam thought about how he could get the ants and bees to help him tunnel into the house. He approached the ants first because they were nearest to him, and because they seemed more friendly. However, when he tried to talk to them he was very frustrated. He found that they simply ignored him. Very politely, he would go up to one ant to explain his problem, but the ant would change directions and walk away. Sam didn't speak "Ant" of course, and so he had no way of knowing that the ants didn't speak "Mouse." Each time the ant changed directions, Sam would move in front of him and squeak just that much louder. Words were spoken, but neither understood the other. Sam next turned to the black bees, who were boring holes in the logs. A mouse can squeeze through a hole the size of a dime, and these bees were boring holes almost as big as the one Sam needed. In trying to talk with the bees, Sam became frustrated. They kept to themselves. They were so busy with their own work that they didn't have time for anyone else.

Sam watched a bee go into a hole and out would come some sawdust, falling directly on Sam's nose. Then the bee would back out and fly off somewhere. It had no time to talk. Sam wasn't even going to learn whether he could talk "Bee" or not. There was no time.

Sam wandered aimlessly through the woodpile, once again alone and discouraged. Then he came upon a large black bee with a broken wing. A broken wing could be fatal for a bee. Unable to go anywhere, this bee was sputtering on the ground. It was obvious to Sam that the bee needed help, even if he couldn't talk with him. In the back of his mind he remembered the old mice who spoke of healing one another. He needed something strong and light to form a splint for the bee's wing. Sam had not listened to their warnings before, but now he would take a chance on their advice. Now a mouse's whiskers are very precious to him. They are like little feelers that enable him to move around in the darkness. Mice have only a few whiskers, so they take good care of them. But Sam was so moved by this large bee struggling to fly that he pulled out one of his whiskers and tied it on the bee's wing to form a splint. Perhaps the real miracle here was that Sam forgot about his own problems. Maybe it was the wonder that is known whenever one sacrifices something precious for the sake of another. All we know is that the bee, who had kicked up a fuss while the splint was being applied, began to understand a language that neither of them had ever used before. The bee tried out his newly repaired wing, hesitantly at first, but with more confidence in every stroke. Soon he was up in the air. He flew out of sight, not even stopping to buzz a "thank you" to his healer. For his part, Sam never had the opportunity to learn to speak "Bee" so he could ask for help properly.

Now, minus one whisker, Sam went back to the house to look for another opening. Staying close to the house, he was muttering something to himself about how foolish it had been to give up a whisker to an ungrateful bee, when he felt sawdust fall on his back. Looking up, he saw a lone, black bee with a mouse whisker splint on its wing, and the bee was carving a hole in the wall, just about the size of a dime.

Chapter 7

Getting back into the house was only the beginning of Sam's troubles. He thought that once he was back in the house everything would go easily. He'd simply talk to the other mice and tell them about the world Outside. They would follow him and that would be that. Of course when he was Outside in the woodpile he also thought that he had it easy then. There always seemed to be something left undone. Planning was new to Sam. Mice don't usually involve themselves in those details. So it was understandable that he might forget something.

Sam was not the mouse he used to be. When Sam left the other mice, he was strong and boastful. Once he had been good-looking as mice go. Now, he didn't look like his former self. His tail was permanently bent by the trap and one of his long beautiful whiskers was missing, giving him an unbalanced look. He was also quite dirty and scratched by his recent entrance into the house by way of a bee hole. He didn't boast anymore about how he could overcome traps, and how Evil was only a relic of history. No, Sam was not the mouse he used to be.

Sam had grown older and a bit more humble from the experience, and at first no one recognized him. Sam had learned how to be patient and slowly the other mice gathered around him to listen to his story. He told them about the place called Outside, about the green grass and the animals that were out there. No one had ever seen a bird before this, and it was hard for them to imagine an animal a hundred times bigger than a fly, floating in the air. He told them about a land of moss and honey. He said that he could lead them there. Eagerly, they started to make preparations. There was another place they could go to escape the house cat that kept them afraid.

"Gather your possessions. Don't take anything you can't easily carry. The way will be narrow and we will have to move quickly if we want to avoid Faro," said Sam.

Faro was the cat. In their excitement the mice had forgotten all about him. Faro had kept the mice in a form of slavery. He pretended to protect them, and even play with them. But when a cat plays with a mouse, the mouse doesn't enjoy it. In the night's darkness Faro crept up on the mice. They ran from him, but every now and then caught one with his paw. When they tried to get away he stopped them. He let them run a little way and then pounce on them. The game of cat and mouse was no fun for the

mouse. When Faro was tired of playing, he would pick up the mouse and carry it away. That mouse was never seen again.

That wasn't all. When Sam showed his fellow mice the narrow exit from the house, another problem presented itself. One mouse named Chucky had grown fat. Chucky said that he was fat because of the cheeses he had found. He had boasted about having found a delicious mozzarella cheese, but one night he had been followed and was found nibbling his way through a box of sugar-coated cereal. Chucky was a junk food addict. All the sugar had made him fat.

All the mice had given him the nick-name of Chunky. A name can be a source of pride or a source of pain. Parents love their children. They spend a great deal of time thinking about what names they want to call them. But mice don't always think about what they are doing. Still, they couldn't leave Chunky to face Faro all by himself. Every mouse agreed, that if Chunky couldn't go no one would go.

How were they going to get Chunky through the narrow bee hole?

Chapter 8

Problems create problems. Because one mouse was too large to fit through a narrow escape hole out of the house all the mice were going to stay with him. Chunky's problem became everyone's problem. There were no two ways about it. Chunky was going to have to lose some weight. Since they didn't have any mouse doctor to talk with about the best way to lose weight, he was immediately put on a starvation diet; no food and lots of exercise. That would mean trouble later on, but mice don't think ahead very well. Chunky exercised each day until he worked up a good mouse sweat. One way or another, those ounces were going to come off.

While Chunky was busy climbing the walls in his exercise course, Sam told the other mice the plan he had worked out to get past Faro, the cat. It was a dangerous plan, but with a little luck they might all get out. One by one the mice would go around the basement room, climb up the concrete block wall, and leave the house through the bee hole.

If Faro came, Sam was going to squeak and distract the cat. When Faro came after him, he was planning to run into a hole. With Faro busy, the other mice would have time to climb up the wall and out the hole. Sam was going to continue to make as much noise as he could, but the others would have to be very quiet so Faro wouldn't hear them. They wouldn't be able to take much with them either. Sam told them the bee hole was going to be a tight squeeze. On the other side of the hole was Outside. He had argued that freedom itself was better and more important than to continue living in fear of Faro. Because each of them had a brother or sister who had been one of Faro's toys, they could only squeak in agreement.

Chunky was tired. He had exercised until he felt his tail would drop off. It had been days since he had eaten any food. The other mice noticed he was having problems and tried to stop Chunky from continuing to lose weight this way. But Chunky was again as thin as the other mice, or so he thought. In any case, they had run out of time.

A month had passed once more. Faro would soon come demanding his mouse meal. Silently they went, one at a time. The oldest mouse went first. Chunky stayed with the younger mice and kept them quiet by telling them stories about what it was going to be like Outside. Since Chunky had never been Outside himself, he was mostly making things up as he went along. He told them that they would have many different kinds of food, including grass and sunflower seeds; how they would bed down each night in nests lined with bird feathers and moss. They would have no worries in this new land of moss and honey. This was to be a heaven on earth. The time came for the young ones to go, and Faro still hadn't appeared. Overconfidence is a bad thing. Chunky had cautioned them all to be quiet, and they were quiet while he was telling the stories, but now they started whispering among themselves about what lay ahead.

The fastest mouse was sent on his way. He raced around the room, behind a cardboard box and up the wall. As he was about to enter the bee hole, he turned back and squeaked to his friends how easy it was. "No problem," he shouted in his loudest squeak.

Only seconds after he had gone into the bee hole, Faro appeared. The fastest one never knew that his words had caused Faro to stir. Faro was sharp-eyed, and he watched the next little mouse run around the room, past the box, up the wall and into the bee hole. Sam saw the danger and squeaked to distract Faro. According to plan, he started running around in circles and making as much noise as one mouse could. Faro, who couldn't keep his eye on two mice, headed for the easiest prey - Sam.

Chapter 9

The mice were trying to get out of the house. Faro, the cat was making it hard for them to escape. It looked like Sam was going to let himself be caught so that the other mice could get away. Sam dove into the hole just behind him, with Faro close on his tail. "This plan will work," thought Sam. He could keep Faro's attention while the other mice made their getaway through the bee hole. One by one the younger mice silently made their way around the room and up the concrete wall to the hole.

Chunky whispered a quick good-bye to all the mice children as he sent them on their way. To each of them he said, "Be silent, go quickly, and I'll see you in the promised land." Even though he spoke encouraging words, Chunky was worried. All his exercising and dieting had been done too quickly and he was one tired mouse.

The last to go was the youngest mouse. He had watched all the others go around the room and climb the wall. "That is a high wall," he thought to himself. "How am I going to make it?" When it was time for him to go, he shared his fears with Chunky. Sometimes when a mouse is afraid, it's good to talk with an older mouse. Chunky was afraid too, but he told the smallest mouse not to worry. Chunky would help him all the way to the bee hole. Helping another is one of the best ways to stop being afraid yourself.

They both ran around the room and up the wall. Chunky followed the little mouse, encouraging him all the way. "Only a little more," he squeaked softly. "Keep on going. You're going to make it."

Meanwhile, Sam was doing his job well. Faro was occupied and didn't see any of the young mice making their escape to the Outside. Anytime Faro seemed to lose interest, Sam would show his face out of the dark hole. Several times, he was almost

caught when he crept out of the hole. It was with much relief that he heard Chunky squeak that all were safe and that he was almost out himself.

Faro heard the squeak too, and he turned just in time to see the youngest mouse make his way into the bee hole. Only Sam and Chunky remained in the house now. With the youngest safely on his way, Chunky climbed the wall toward the safety of the hole. He panicked. He hadn't lost enough ounces; he was still too big to fit through the hole. Tired and weak as he was from his dieting, Chunky lost his grip on the wall and fell to the floor with a soft thud. Luckily, he fell on top of a cardboard box and wasn't hurt.

With Faro's back turned, Sam tried to make his own escape. The plan called for Sam to lure Faro over to the wood and steel trap that had been reset and was once again giving off deadly aromas. In the darkness, and with a little bit of luck, Sam hoped to get Faro to step on the trap, then he would make his escape. That which was evil was going to trap another form of evil. Sam raced through the room straight toward the trap with Faro right behind him. Neither one noticed Chunky lying on the box.

Now it was a race. "When your life depends on it, you can race the devil himself," Sam thought, and so it seemed to him. Just as Faro was closing in on him, Sam reached the trap and leaped over it. Alas, there was a flaw in the plan. Faro knew about the trap too, and he simply stepped over it. Now, at the base of the wall, Faro had Sam trapped.

Chapter 10

The best laid plans of men and mice often go wrong. Sam thought Faro, the cat, would be trapped by the same mouse trap that had once caught him. However, what is a trap for one creature is not a trap for another. Meanwhile Chunky recovered from his fall off the wall and quickly saw the trouble before him. He saw that Faro was going to get a mouse after all. It seemed very likely that Sam was going to be that mouse.

Faro hadn't noticed Chunky. If he lay very still, maybe he could still escape later, but if Chunky distracted Faro, maybe Sam could get away. Either way, one of them was going to be cat food.

Chunky didn't know what to do. Earlier Sam had told the mice that it had hurt when he had given up his whisker to help a bee, but that it would have hurt even more if he hadn't made the sacrifice. Chunky's decision wasn't about a mere whisker, it was about life itself. He had to choose between losing his friend or losing his own life.

Then Chunky knew what he had to do. When he thought only about himself, he was the loser; he was controlled by fear. When he thought about how he could help Sam, he didn't feel afraid. He didn't even feel sorry for himself.

Chunky made his decision. Making as much noise as he could, he stood up and ran down the box. Faro looked around. "I'm the one you want Faro," squeaked the still fat mouse, "but you won't be able to catch me."

Tired and bruised from his fall, Chunky crawled into the middle of the room. Faro couldn't resist Chunky's taunts, and he bounded after him. In three steps, Faro had Chunky within his grasp; he began to play with his prey before making the final, deadly blow. Faro had a living toy, and he meant to make the most of it.

Sam realized that he had a duty to help the other mice who depended on him, and he ran up the wall and out the bee hole. He glanced back at his friend who was about to give up his life to save him. One large mouse tear fell to the floor.

Chapter 11

Sam paused at the entrance to the Outside world. His friend Chunky, was being pawed by the cat and there was nothing he could do to save him.

The bee hole was very small, and Sam didn't have an easier time getting out than he had getting in. He couldn't help thinking about Chunky who he had just left behind. "Chunky had only thought about himself before. He might not have been much of a mouse," thought Sam. "He once bragged about all the different kinds of cheeses he was eating, but never offered to share them. Then we discovered that the cheese he was talking about was actually a sugar-coated cereal. Why is he giving up his life for me? A mouse has to have a great love in his heart to be able to give up his life for someone else," Sam thought sadly. He wondered if he could be so generous with his own life. He decided that he would never know for certain unless a mouse he knew and loved was in danger.

Sam climbed slowly down the wall Outside where all the other mice were waiting for him. They were expecting Sam to come out after Chunky. All the mice asked where Chunky was, especially the younger mice whom he had watched over so carefully. Sam told them how Chunky had come back to help him avoid Faro, and slowly added that Chunky wouldn't be with them any more.

It was a very sad tribe of mice who made their way to the woodpile that day. They hardly noticed the green grass, the trees, and the sky overhead. Just as Sam had discovered earlier, these mice learned that a house is only a place to live. It is the ones you love who make it a home. They couldn't bear to look back at the house that had been their home. They could only think about Chunky. So it was a complete surprise to them when they saw Chunky running toward them. He had been hopelessly trapped. How had he escaped from Faro?

Chapter 12

Looking back over his shoulder fearfully, Chunky ran toward the band of mice. Somehow he had managed to escape from the cat. No one knew how he managed to do it. But there he was. When he arrived at the woodpile, he almost collapsed. There were scratches on his sides, and he was out of breath.

Chunky squeaked out his story a little bit at a time. He remembered being in the middle of the floor while Faro toyed with him. Faro had pulled in his claws and was batting him around the floor. Chunky knew it was only going to be a matter of time before Faro gave the final blow. When he saw Sam disappear into the escape hole, he felt totally alone. Chunky felt small and very helpless. He decided to roll himself into a ball. Then he squeezed his eyes shut and said a little prayer thanking God for allowing him to help his friends go free.

The next thing he knew, Faro gave a loud "Meow." Chunky opened his eyes. Standing before him was a large Being many times greater than Faro. (As Chunky spoke, Sam remembered a Great Being in his past too. Could it be the same Being who had brought Sam out to the woodpile when he was caught in a trap?)

Chunky continued. "This Being reached down and picked up Faro with one hand. We thought Faro was all powerful. We were afraid of him," he exclaimed, "but this Being picked up Faro with ease. I opened one eye and saw the Great Being's other hand pull a round handle on the wall. As he pulled, a section of the wall moved, and I saw the green grass and sky and you running to this woodpile. The Being held the wall open, and I ran out as fast as I could."

The other mice cheered and could hardly stop talking among themselves. They began calling him Chucky again. They couldn't tease him anymore with a fat nickname. Chucky's love had made him brave. The mice couldn't bring themselves to tease someone

who loved them. No one could keep silent, but Chucky quieted them. He had more to tell them. They weren't safe yet. The Great Being had said, "Run far away little one; Faro will be outside tonight."

Shivers ran up and down the backs of all the mice. The bright light in the sky was slipping behind the horizon. Faro would be coming soon.

Chapter 13

Night was coming. The tribe of mice who left the house they had lived in for generations were beginning to sense that there were new dangers that came with their new home in the Outside world. The cat they had left behind was now on their trail.

Sam, who had been there before, knew that Outside would be dark soon. When he heard the words of warning about the cat he couldn't stop to think about the Great Being who had released him from a trap and who had enabled Chucky to escape a certain death, but there were some questions in the back of his mind. Was this Great Being also responsible for keeping the cat and setting the traps? Was this Great Being a friend or an enemy?

There were a great many things Sam didn't know; like how houses were built, or why there were woodpiles. Sam just took these things for granted. There were questions entering his mind now, ones he had even taken the time to think about before. What had made Chucky willing to give up his life for another mouse? This was the same Chucky who never before even shared his food with anyone. How had Chucky come to be so brave?

There was no time to think about that. The mice simply had to move to another place where they wouldn't need to fear traps and cats. Sam had promised the rest of the mice that being Outside would be better than being in the house. Now he would fulfill that promise. Together, they set out from the woodpile and scurried through the grass.

Soon they came to what looked like a row of small, flat trees. The trees were lined up close to one another, and they had no branches or leaves. They were so close together that the mice were sure that Faro couldn't possibly squeeze between them. They would be safe on the other side of the wooden fence. They didn't realize that whatever kept Faro out also might be keeping something else in.

Chapter 14

An escape from one danger was bringing the mice to face another unknown. They left the house to live in a woodpile. But since that wasn't going to be far enough away to be out of the reach of Faro the cat, they left the yard.

After all the mice pushed themselves through the narrow openings of the fence, they felt safe. As they walked on, in the fading daylight, they didn't notice a pair of eyes watching them. The eyes belonged to a large dog who lived in the yard where the mice had fled. Her owners called her "Big Red." They had placed a large sign in the yard saying, "Beware of Dog." Mice, however, can't read "human" language, so the sign didn't mean anything to them. As dogs go, Big Red was rather friendly. She would bark at passing cars, but when people passed by, Red simply wagged her tail. Red's owners had been hoping for a watchdog, but Red refused to cooperate. Red just wanted to be friendly.

In spite of her refusal to be a vicious watchdog, Red was tied to a stake with a long rope. "If Red wasn't really dangerous," her owners reasoned, "at least she was going to look dangerous." Big Red was one unhappy dog. Tied to the stake, she was unable to make friends with anyone.

When the mice started through the yard, Red thought she saw a chance to make new friends, and she lunged toward them. Red didn't have much experience at making friends. The mice were frightened, but when Big Red reached the end of her rope, she stopped and all she did was wag her tail.

As Big Red calmed down, the mice came up and stood near her. She slowly wagged her tail some more. What could a large dog tied to a stake do for a band of mice, and what could they do for her?

Chapter 15

While the mice stood just outside the reach of Big Red, they hadn't noticed additional company coming up behind them. Faro!! Big Red started to bark.

Faro wasn't about to be kept from the mice by a simple wooden fence. With one mighty leap, the cat sprang to the top of the fence and then down on the other side. One loud "Meow" announced his coming. He knew Big Red was tied. More than once he sat outside the brown circle that Red had made in the grass when she was pacing, and teased her. Now Faro had all the mice trapped in an open yard.

Big Red was the first to notice Faro, because she was looking in that direction. When the mice realized that she wasn't barking at them, they turned and saw their old enemy creeping up on

RE

them. With Faro on one side and Big Red barking on the other, what could they do?

Sam had to think fast. He was responsible for getting his family and friends into trouble, and he was going to get them out of it. "Everyone run to the little house at the other end of the rope." Sam shouted. The mice raced to a small wooden shelter in the middle of Red's circle.

Red's full concentration was on Faro. "If only I were free from my rope, that cat would never come into my yard again to tease me," she thought.

The tribe of mice was safe, at least for the moment, but they were also trapped. Red would make Faro keep his distance, but there was nothing for them to eat within that circle, no berries, grass seed or anything else that looked edible. This was not what they had been promised when they agreed to leave the house.

Mice usually don't think that they can do very much. From their point of view, everyone else is very big and able to do a great deal more than they can do. The oldest mice had said that the Great Being had built the world where they lived all their lives. What could a small band of mice do in comparison to the Great Being? Perhaps, if they squeaked loud enough, the Great Being would come to their rescue as he had before. But in spite of all their sounds, no Great Being came to help them. "Where is this Being when we need him?" they grumbled, and they turned their attention to their empty stomachs.

When a mouse is hungry he might eat anything in front of him. These mice were no different. Chucky was hungry too, and convinced himself that the rope that held Big Red to the stake might be edible. On his advice, and because there was nothing else to do, the mice started chewing on it.

Chapter 16

Trapped in a dog house is not much different than being trapped in any other house, except there was nothing to eat. Big Red was keeping the cat away from them, but who was going to keep Big Red away. Can the enemy of an enemy be trusted as a friend?

The mice had no possessions, no food, and nowhere to go, but they did have one ability that could save them if they knew how to use it: they could chew. They started gnawing at the rope, which held Red in the yard.

As ropes go, it wasn't particularly tasty, and it had been dragged around in the dirt for a long time, but because they were hungry, the mice chewed it anyway. It wasn't long until the rope broke and Big Red was free. The dog had not been free for a long time. Before, the rope had always stopped her. She had even learned to use the rope to balance herself when she stood on her back legs. When at the end of her rope, Big Red would lean forward and the rope kept her standing. This time, however, the rope didn't hold her and Big Red fell to the ground.

Her paws were on the grass outside the dirt circle. Years of pacing in a confined space marked a well defined area to both cat and dog. As long as Faro stayed on the green he was safe. He was so close to danger and so safe, much to Big Red's frustration, which she expressed with constant barking. Big Red was surprised, but only for a moment. The new reality of freedom became clear to both animals at the same time. Now it was Faro who turned and ran across the yard and up, over the line of small flat boards with Big Red following close behind. The mice, doubting that they could ever be friends with Big Red because of her size, ran in the opposite direction.

Future generations of mice would tell stories about the house they once lived in, about Faro the cat, how Sam had been trapped and broke his tail, and about how Chucky had offered his life so that his friend could be free. Then they would add the story about being trapped by the cat and how their own hunger freed a large dog who saved them.

The mice were so busy telling each other their stories that they forgot about their hunger. Getting the stories straight, caused a great deal of squeaking. They were all involved in the same event, but each saw it from a different viewpoint. It was the old story of three blind mice examining an ice cube on a warm summer day. The first one who came upon it went back and told his two friends that it was like a hard, cold block. The next one went to see for himself what it was like and returned to say that it was not at all hard, but was a flat puddle that one could drink from. The third, wanting to resolve the difference between the first two mice, went to examine it for himself, but returned saying he searched everywhere, and found nothing, except, he noticed, that the air seemed humid. Each mouse was sure he had the true story of what they had experienced. In the end, they simply decided to tell all the stories.

For the first time in their lives the mice didn't feel the need to sneak out and to run from one hiding place to another. They were free at last! The experiences they shared brought them closer together. Telling stories about their experiences brought this small tribe of mice even closer together. For the first time, they were truly free.

What would they do with that freedom! Is it possible that the experiences which brought them together would also separate them?

Chapter 17

When everything is going right, mice don't think about narrow escapes. Finally, they were free from their past, or so they thought. They managed to get out of a house, escape a cat and a dog. They were free and making up stories about their own imagined bravery. The little tribe of mice marched off together under the moonlight down the middle of a road. They were brave. They were fearless. Had they not defeated Faro? Had they not come through the valley of the shadow of death itself? "No one can conquer us," they shouted. "We have Sam the Wise as our leader, and with him is Chucky the Brave."

This was good to hear, but Sam wasn't feeling very wise and Chucky, who was glad to be rid of his other nickname, still had day-mares (because he slept during the day) about his encounters with Faro.

No matter how brave and wise a mouse feels it is never a good idea to forget common sense. Walking down the middle of a road isn't something even brave and wise mice should do.

One of the smaller mice was the first to notice what looked like two bright stars close to the road that seemed to be growing bigger. He had never seen stars before, and these were coming toward them. He pointed them out to his parents. The mice were amazed by the bright lights, and they pointed them out to each other. In what seemed like no time at all, the stars were casting a bright light on the brave band of mice. They raced toward the light.

For some reason, at that moment, Sam remembered the feelings he had now, were the same feelings he had just before the steel trap had caught him by the tail. "It's another . . . ." Sam didn't finish his sentence. The sound of a roaring wind came upon them, and the lights swept over them.

Chapter 18

It only looked like two stars on the ground coming toward the mouse tribe, or so they thought. Each territory has its own dangers. Dangers aren't so frightening once we have learned how to deal with them. It is only when they are new and we don't know what to expect, that simple problems may be dangerous.

A car swept over the mice, crushing a few and scattering the rest in the wind like so many leaves. Disaster had come upon them so suddenly that they could hardly believe it. They were dazed and confused. As they gathered themselves together, another tragedy came upon them.

An owl, who had been watching them with curiosity, was hungry for a meal of fresh mouse. Long, silent strokes of his wings, lifted the owl off the branch overhead. In an instant there was one less mouse on the ground.

Now confusion gave way to anger. "Why did we come out here?" they shouted. "We will all surely be killed in this place just as we were in the house. At least there we knew what to expect. If we had stayed in the house, maybe we could have been friends with Faro. Faro wasn't a bad cat after all. He even liked to play with us."

When they are afraid, mice sometimes stretch their imaginations to make the bad look good. Mice also squeak a great deal when faced with the unknown. To them, new dangers always seem worse than old ones. The mice might have gone back to the house had it not been for one of the mice children, who, with one question caused all the adult mice to forget about ever going back to the house. With his one question he would enable his elders to face all the hardships and trials that awaited them.

Chapter 19

One question. When new troubles make the journey difficult mice may forget why they started it in the first place. In such times they need to be reminded of their original purpose. One small mouse remembered what the adult mice forgot. He reminded them of that purpose by asking one question.

The little mouse looked at Sam and asked, "If we go back, will we still be free in the house?"

All the mice knew the answer to this question. They remembered that freedom was their goal for leaving the house. The paradise they were seeking was not a place of comfort but a land where they could be free. The mice gathered their courage together. "We are free," they shouted, "and we will stay free!"

They remembered how both Sam had been freed from the trap and Chucky had escaped with the help of the Great Being. While they couldn't see the Great Being they felt that they were not alone in their journey to freedom.

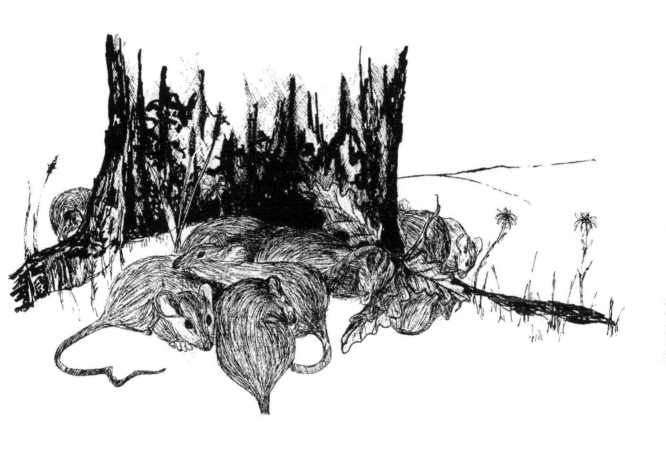

Sam hoped and doubted at the same time. He remembered the wisdom of ancient generations that he had cast aside to yield to a trap's tempting aroma. "Each of us learns in his own way," he thought. "Experience will make us learn lessons from the past when we choose to ignore them."

The morning light found the band of mice weary and worn. The mouse tribe slept at the base of a tree cloaked in a pile of leaves, without knowing where they were going to sleep the next day. In the distance, beyond their sight, was an old deserted barn where a black carpenter bee with a mouse whisker for a splint on its wing was carving out a hole the size of a dime.

BUT THAT'S ANOTHER STORY